Friendship Dance

Twink

Bimi

Pix

Sooze

Sili

Mariella

Kiki

Ivy

Book Eleven

Friendship Dance

Titania Woods
Illustrated by Smiljana Coh

BLOOMSBURY

LONDON BERLIN NEW YORK

Bloomsbury Publishing, London, Berlin and New York

First published in Great Britain in 2009 by Bloomsbury Publishing Plc
36 Soho Square, London, W1D 3QY

A CIP catalogue record of this book is available from the British Library

ISBN 978 0 7475 9833 6

All papers used by Bloomsbury Publishing are natural, recyclable products made
from wood grown in well-managed forests. The manufacturing processes conform to
the environmental regulations of the country of origin.

Typeset by Dorchester Typesetting Group Ltd
Printed in Singapore by Tien Wah Press

1 3 5 7 9 10 8 6 4 2

www.glitterwingsacademy.co.uk

To Linda C.

Chapter One

Twink Flutterby and her friends sat perched on mushroom seats in the Great Branch, waiting for Miss Shimmery, their HeadFairy, to address the school.

Twink smiled happily as she looked around her at the other fairies. A new autumn term! She had had a good summer holiday, but it was glimmery to be back at Glitterwings Academy. The oak tree school felt like home.

'I wonder what Miss Shimmery's announcement is going to be?' whispered Bimi Bluebell, her best

friend. Both girls were sitting at the Violet Branch table. Other tables in the Great Branch had different flowers hanging over them, so that the long, spacious Branch looked like a colourful garden.

Twink shrugged. 'The usual, I suppose – uniforms from tomorrow, and no high-speed flying!'

Her friend Sooze leaned across the mossy table with a grin. 'Haven't you heard, then, Opposite? Miss Twilight said there's something special Miss Shimmery is going to tell us!' Sooze had lavender hair and pink wings – the exact *opposite* of Twink.

Twink's eyes widened. 'No, I hadn't heard that! I wonder what –'

She broke off as Miss Shimmery herself appeared, hovering over the platform at the front of the Branch. 'Welcome!' said their HeadFairy, her rainbow wings glinting like opals. 'It's good to see everyone back. I've just a few things to tell you . . .'

Twink fidgeted as Miss Shimmery made all the announcements she'd predicted, and a few other ordinary ones besides: no bothering the water sprites in the school pond, oak-leaf caps required at

all times . . . oh, when would she get to the interesting bit?

Suddenly Twink sat up straight. Miss Shimmery was taking her sparkle specs off! She only ever did that when she had something important to say.

The HeadFairy regarded the school with a slight smile. 'Finally, I've a rather special announcement to make. As you may be aware, it's our beloved Queen's five-hundredth birthday in two weeks. There is, naturally, going to be a great celebration to commemorate this – and a student from Glitterwings Academy will be taking part in it.'

Twink and her friends glanced at each other, startled. None of them had dreamed the announcement might be something like this! The school waited breathlessly for Miss Shimmery to explain.

'Fairies from seven other schools will be involved as well,' continued Miss Shimmery, her snowy hair gleaming. 'Together, the eight students will perform the traditional Friendship Dance at Queen Mab's birthday celebrations.'

A thrill ran across Twink's wings. Who would the lucky student from Glitterwings be? One of the older girls, certainly. She twisted on her seat to look at the upper-year tables.

'I bet it'll be Poppy Greenwing,' said Bimi in Twink's ear. 'She's the best dancer in the school!'

Speculations buzzed about the Branch like bees. Poppy, sitting with the Sixth Years, seemed to think it might be her as well. Her cheeks were pink, and all her friends were whispering excitedly to her.

Miss Shimmery went on as if she hadn't noticed the stir her words had caused. 'Now, of course, for such an important event, we must make sure that we choose the right student. The Friendship Dance creates a very strong magic. Which student will fit into that magic the best, and bring something to it that's needed?'

Twink frowned, uncertain what the HeadFairy meant. She made it sound like it wasn't about dancing at all.

Reaching into a small pouch at her hip, Miss Shimmery drew out a bright, gleaming orb. A murmur of surprise ran through the school.

'A sparkle-seeker,' confirmed Miss Shimmery, holding it up. It shone in her hand like a tiny star. 'We cannot leave this matter to chance; there are too many variables to consider. And so the sparkle-seeker will tell us which student to send.'

Twink gazed at the glowing ball in wonder. She had never seen a sparkle-seeker before; they were normally only used for solemn decisions concerning adults. This dance must be very important indeed!

With a flurry of her long sleeve, Miss Shimmery tossed the sparkle-seeker into the air. It hovered in place for a moment . . . and then slowly flew out into the Branch.

The fairies held their breath as the shining light circled this way and that. Sometimes it hesitated at a table, but it always moved on again, floating lazily about the room.

Poppy sat watching anxiously, but the glowing orb flew past her without even pausing. Twink and Bimi looked at each other, their eyebrows raised. If not Poppy, then who?

Sooze gasped. 'It's heading this way!'

As Twink and her friends watched open-mouthed, the sparkle-seeker drifted towards them. It was even brighter up close: a tiny, pulsating whiteness. It circled the Violet Branch table as the fairies sat very still, hardly daring to move.

It stopped over Twink's head.

Twink peered up in confusion, waiting for the star to move on. But it stayed where it was, gently turning. Amazed whispers burst out across the Branch.

'Twink!' hissed Bimi, grabbing Twink's arm. 'It's chosen *you*!'

'But –' Twink could hardly speak. Her face felt on fire. The sparkle-seeker *couldn't* have chosen her. Why on earth would it?

'Twink, please come forward,' said Miss Shimmery.

In a daze Twink fluttered to the front of the Great Branch, with the star bobbing along after her. Surely there had been some sort of error, and Miss Shimmery was going to tell everyone so and try again?

Instead, the HeadFairy smiled warmly at her. 'The sparkle-seeker has chosen,' she said. 'Well done, Twink.'

'But – but Miss Shimmery, this has to be a mistake,' stammered Twink. 'I'm only a third-year student!'

Miss Shimmery shook her head. 'Age has nothing to do with it. You'll bring something to the dance that is needed, and that no other student can bring. Now, with your permission, I'll write to your parents this evening by special night-moth. If they say yes, then you'll leave for the palace tomorrow.

You'll stay there for two weeks, to practise the dance and then perform it at the celebrations.'

Two weeks? Twink opened her mouth and shut it again. But that was so long!

'Only if you agree, though,' said Miss Shimmery gently. 'Are you willing to go to the palace and represent our school, Twink?'

Twink's thoughts tumbled like autumn leaves. Go to the palace and dance for Queen Mab? On the one wing, it sounded like the most thrilling thing in the world . . . but on the other, it sounded more than a little scary. Just a few minutes ago, she had been looking forward to a nice, ordinary term with her friends – and now this!

Biting her lip in uncertainty, she looked out at the school. At the Snowdrop Branch table, her younger sister Teena was staring at her wide-eyed. And a few tables along, Twink's friends were smiling broadly at her. 'Say *yes*, Twink!' came Sooze's piercing whisper.

Laughter rippled across the Branch. Even Miss Shimmery smiled. 'Well?' she asked.

Twink took a deep breath. Above her, the star still

shone, casting a bright light across her features. 'All right,' she said. 'I'll do it!'

Twink's parents gave their permission gladly, and a few hours later, Twink found herself repacking her oak-leaf bag. It felt very strange to be the only fairy packing!

'Twink, you're so lucky!' breathed a pointy-faced fairy called Mariella. 'Imagine going to the palace! Of course,' she added, flipping back her silvery-green hair, 'my parents are *very* close to Queen Mab, so *I* wouldn't be that impressed . . . but you must be over the moon!'

Twink hid a smile. It was just as well that Sooze hadn't overheard, or she'd have teased Mariella about her grandmother, who had been one of the Queen's cleaning fairies.

'*Are* you excited, Twink?' asked Bimi when it was time for glow-worms out. She and Twink were sleeping in the larger of the two loft-spaces in Violet Branch this term, along with a clever fairy called Pix.

Twink sighed, snuggling down into her mossy

bed. Her oak-leaf bag sat on the floor beside her, packed and ready for the journey the next morning. At her side, her bedside mushroom looked bare and empty.

'Yes, of course,' said Twink. 'It's just . . . well, I'm going to miss everyone, that's all. Two weeks is *ages*.'

'I know,' said Bimi sympathetically. 'We'll miss you too, Twink . . . especially me! But you'll have a brilliant time. The two weeks will fly past!'

'And it's not like you could really say no,' pointed out Pix drowsily from the next bed. 'Imagine it – *Sorry, Your Majesty, but I'm too busy at school to dance at your party. Maybe next time!*'

The three fairies giggled. Pix was right, thought Twink. She *had* to agree to such an important event, whether she'd miss Glitterwings or not.

But maybe the time would pass quickly, as Bimi had said. Twink hoped so. Going to the palace sounded glimmery . . . but not as glimmery as being with her friends.

Chapter
Two

Early the next morning, Twink set off with Miss Shimmery to make the long journey to the palace. A large brown hawk stood outside the tree waiting to carry them.

Twink gulped when she saw that the entire school had assembled on the front lawn to wave her off. She was glad that she'd already said a private goodbye to her friends and Teena – it would be impossible now, in front of such a crowd!

'Three cheers for Twink!' bellowed Madge, the school Games Captain.

'Hip, hip, hooray!' chanted all the students, clapping their wings together. 'Hip, hip, hooray!'

Twink's cheeks burned. She could hardly even look at poor Poppy, standing with the upper years! 'Miss Shimmery, are you *sure* the sparkle-seeker didn't make a mistake?' she whispered as they settled on to the hawk's smooth, muscular back.

'Quite sure!' laughed Miss Shimmery.

The hawk took off with a sudden rush of wings. Glitterwings grew smaller and smaller below them, until its autumn leaves were only a brightly coloured dot on a miniature green hill.

'Don't worry, Twink,' added the HeadFairy, looking over her shoulder. 'The sparkle-seeker knows things we can't see. There's a reason you were chosen, I promise you.'

It still seemed very strange to Twink, but if Miss Shimmery was satisfied, then she supposed she should be, too. Meanwhile, the autumn morning was crisp and sunny – a perfect day for a flight. Twink gave herself over to enjoying the rhythm of the hawk's wing strokes, and the cool tickle of the

breeze in her hair.

Even so, the flight took a long time, and Twink was relieved when Miss Shimmery finally pointed to a lush wood in the distance. 'That's Royal Wood. The palace is right in the centre of it – there, in that clearing!'

Twink blinked as the hawk glided downward. Why, this was just an ordinary clearing, with a few spreading bushes in it. Where was the palace?

The bird touched down with a graceful hop, and Twink and Miss Shimmery flew off his back,

landing on the grass beside him. Immediately, a portly fairy with light blue wings came fluttering over.

'Madame Shimmery!' he cried, clicking his heels together and kissing Miss Shimmery's hand.

Madame Shimmery? Twink stifled a giggle.

'Maximus, how lovely to see you,' said Miss Shimmery. 'And may I introduce Twink Flutterby, the Glitterwings student who is to take part in the celebrations?'

'Welcome, Miss Flutterby,' said Maximus solemnly, clicking his heels again. 'We are honoured to have you here.'

'Thank you,' said Twink. She clutched her bag to her chest. 'I – I'm honoured to be here.'

All too soon, Miss Shimmery was saying goodbye. 'I'll be back for the celebrations, my dear,' she said, squeezing Twink's shoulder. 'Good luck – I'm sure you'll do splendidly!'

'Goodbye, Miss Shimmery,' said Twink, trying to smile. But as she watched her HeadFairy fly away on the hawk, she rather wished that she *had* told

Queen Mab she was too busy to come!

'Come along now, Miss Flutterby,' said Maximus, taking Twink's bag from her. 'I'll show you where you and the other girls are staying. That will be nice, won't it?'

'Er – yes,' said Twink. 'I mean . . . thank you.' Oh, great – Maximus sounded as if he thought Twink was still in acorn school!

The chubby fairy led the way to the largest of the spreading bushes. 'But where's the palace?' asked Twink in confusion.

Maximus gave her a haughty glance. 'Right here!' he announced.

Passing through a low archway formed by the bush's bottom branches, he disappeared within its foliage. Twink followed . . . and caught her breath. The inside of the bush was the most amazing residence she'd ever seen!

Queen Mab's palace wasn't just one building, it was *hundreds*. They were like human tree houses, only these were fairy-sized, and covered every level of the bush for as far up as Twink could see. They had sparkling windows, and towers and turrets, and were every shape and size imaginable.

Maximus almost seemed to smile at Twink's dazed expression. 'Come along, Miss Flutterby,' he urged. 'It will be time for your first dance lesson soon.'

He fluttered upwards, leading Twink through a complicated maze of branches and buildings. *I'll never remember how to get there!* thought Twink. She hung back shyly as a pair of richly-dressed fairies swooped past, deep in conversation.

'Here we are – Sapphire Room,' announced Maximus at last. Landing in front of a large circular tree house, he knocked briskly on the door. A chorus of giggles came from inside.

'Come in!' called a merry voice.

Looking disapproving, Maximus pushed open the door and motioned for Twink to enter. She did so – and her mouth fell open. The room was decorated with real sapphires! The glittering gems were every-where, shining like pieces of deep blue sky.

Three other fairies were in the room, watching her curiously.

'Miss Flutterby, may I introduce Miss Sunlight, Miss Lavender and Miss Wintersong,' said Maximus. 'Young ladies, please make Miss Flutterby feel welcome. I'll be back soon to collect all of you for your first dance rehearsal.' Handing Twink her oak-leaf bag, Maximus departed.

A fairy with bright yellow hair and orange wings flitted over. 'Hi, I'm Tilli – *Miss Sunlight*, that is!' She grinned. 'And these two are really called Jena and Snow.'

'I'm Jena,' put in a tiny fairy with purple hair. She was sitting cross-legged on her bed examining herself in a mirror, but she looked up and smiled.

'And I'm Snow!' laughed the last girl. She had snowy-white hair and dark eyes, and wore the leafy Sparklelight uniform.

'What's your name?' continued Tilli. 'When you're not busy being *Miss Flutterby*, that is!'

Twink grinned at them, hugely relieved that she wasn't going to have to call everyone *Miss* for two weeks! 'I'm Twink,' she said, dropping her bag on the last empty bed. Its carved wooden headboard

glittered with sapphires.

'Are you from Glitterwings?' asked Jena, putting away her mirror.

Twink nodded. 'How about all of you? You're from Sparklelight, aren't you?' she added eagerly to Snow. 'Our Fledge team played there last year. Your school is really pretty!' The Sparklelight campus was set behind a woodland waterfall, with sunlight dancing through the curtain of water.

Snow beamed. 'Oh, thanks! *We* like it. And I've heard that Glitterwings is really glimmery, too.'

'I go to Forestglow,' said Jena, rooting about in her bedside drawer. She pulled out a hair clasp. 'It's OK, but I'm going to try and change to Sparklelight for my last year. I'm studying Fairy Dust, and Sparklelight has a brilliant course.'

Twink's eyes widened. Despite her diminutive size, Jena was clearly several years older than the rest of them. The purple-haired fairy had an air of confidence about her, as if she knew exactly what she wanted.

'And I go to Emerald Leaf,' grimaced Tilli. 'Yes, I

know, go on and say it! They're all stuck-up little beetles there.'

Twink burst out laughing. There was an ornate wooden cabinet next to her bed, and she began to unpack her belongings into it. 'Well, I *have* heard that,' she admitted. 'Is Emerald Leaf really that bad?'

'Worse!' said Tilli dramatically, flinging herself on to her bed. 'There are only one or two *normal* fairies in the whole school. Everyone else is always talking about who their families know, and how terribly, terribly important they are . . . ugh!'

'It sounds awful,' said Twink, liking the brightly coloured fairy already. 'Can't you change schools? There's a girl in my branch who used to go to Emerald Leaf, and she's much happier at Glitterwings.'

'Oh, who?' asked Tilli, sitting up. When Twink told her, she grinned. 'Kiki! She was in the year below me; we used to have really good moans together over how miserable we both were. Well, I'm glad she's better off now!'

'But why can't you change schools too?' asked Snow. The white-haired fairy was exploring the common area of their room, peering into sparkling sapphire cupboards and sliding open drawers.

Tilli sighed. 'Oh, I don't know. My mother went to Emerald Leaf, and my aunt's a teacher there. They both seem really set on my sticking it out.'

'That's too bad,' said Twink sympathetically. She unpacked her petal books, along with a small box of fairy dust that she had brought along to practise with. Her teachers had all given her work to do while she was away, and Twink was determined that she wasn't going to fall behind.

Jena pulled her purple hair back into a ponytail. 'Yes, but Emerald Leaf is still an excellent school, Tilli,' she pointed out. 'So at least you'll get a good education.'

Snow gaped at her in horror. 'But we don't just go to school to *learn*, we go to make friends, too! And anyway, Tilli, if you do change schools, you should go to Sparklelight, because – oh, look!' Snow interrupted herself as she opened a little box. 'Sapphire

earrings!' She dangled them in front of her ears with a pout, and everyone laughed.

'Do you know why you were chosen for the Friendship Dance, Twink?' asked Jena. She tied a violet ribbon around her ponytail.

Twink shook her head. 'My school used a sparkle-seeker, but I think it must have made a mistake,' she admitted. 'I don't see how *I* can bring anything to the dance.'

'None of us know why we were chosen either,'

said Tilli. 'But I'm glad I was. A two-week holiday from Emerald Leaf, hurrah!' She punched the air.

'I wonder what the boys will be like?' said Snow. She bounced on to her bed, still playing with the earrings.

'Boys?' Twink stopped unpacking and stared at her.

'Yes, didn't you know?' said Jena. She pulled on a pair of bright red pixie boots. 'The Friendship Dance is done with partners – four boys and four girls.'

'No, I – I didn't know that,' said Twink. *Boys?*

Slowly, she placed a drawing of her family on the cabinet beside her bed. Twink had never really spoken to a boy her own age – and wasn't at all sure how she felt about dancing with one! Why couldn't the dance be just girls?

Snow nodded enthusiastically. 'I saw them earlier, when Maximus was taking them to their room. One of them is *really* swoony!'

Swoony? Twink wrinkled her nose in disgust. Snow couldn't be serious!

Tilli's yellow eyebrows were raised. She and Twink exchanged a glance, and burst into giggles.

'What?' demanded Snow, propping her hands on her hips. 'He *is* swoony, wait and see! He's got green hair and purple wings, and –'

There was a knock at the door. 'Time for your first practice, girls,' called Maximus. 'Top of the palace, immediately!'

'We're almost ready,' returned Jena calmly. 'Come on, you lot, hurry,' she added, inspecting herself in her mirror.

Suddenly Twink realised that while the rest of them had just been chatting, Jena had been quietly getting ready! Along with Tilli and Snow, she scrambled to comb her hair and smooth her dress.

'*Young ladies*, I must insist on promptness!' huffed Maximus from the other side of the door.

Jena ignored him, snapping her mirror shut. 'All right?' she asked, giving them all a quick once-over. She smiled. 'Then let's go and show those boys what we're made of!'

Chapter
Three

Twink and the other girls followed Maximus up through the winding branches. The higher they flew, the more elaborate the buildings became. Windows and jewels sparkled everywhere, and there were carvings of fairies and woodland creatures.

A leaf brushed Twink's face as she flitted under a branch. The bush was dense with foliage, yet sunlight danced all around them. *It must be magic*, thought Twink.

Suddenly she stopped, staring upwards. A small, shadowy figure was peering at her from behind a

nearby leaf. As Twink gaped back at it, an important-looking fairy flew past, and whoever it was ducked quickly out of sight.

'Come along, now!' called Maximus. 'We have a *schedule*, Miss Flutterby!'

With a start, Twink hastened to catch up with the others. Glancing over her shoulder, she saw only leaves and branches. *I probably just imagined it*, she thought with a frown.

The fairies landed in a wide courtyard. To one side rose the grandest building yet, rising up through the branches and leaves. Twink's eyes widened as she took it in. This was clearly where Queen Mab herself lived.

Four boys stood waiting in the centre of the courtyard, each wearing a different school uniform. Twink thought they looked just as curious about the girls as they were about them!

'This courtyard is where we shall practise; it is also where the birthday celebrations will take place,' announced Maximus. With a wave of his hand, he introduced the two groups at lightning speed.

'Misses Flutterby, Sunlight, Wintersong and Lavender, may I present Masters Halcyon, Sparkworth, Greenbranch and Moss. Now, please line up so that I can put you in pairs.'

Her head spinning, Twink lined up with the others. Tilli nudged her. 'I hope you paid attention,' she whispered. 'There's going to be a test later.'

Twink smiled, and then quickly stood up straight as Maximus pointed at her. 'Miss Flutterby, please come forward. And you, Master Greenbranch.'

Feeling very self-conscious, Twink stepped away from the line of fairies. Master Greenbranch turned out to be a boy with bright green hair and purple wings. Maximus fussed around the two of them, moving them this way and that.

'Hmm,' he said, squinting his eyes in thought.

Twink and the boy exchanged a bewildered glance. Master Greenbranch looked as if he were trying not to laugh, and Twink bit her lip to hold back her own giggle.

'No, that won't do at all,' said Maximus suddenly. He motioned the green-haired boy back with the

others. 'Master Sparkworth, please.'

A boy about Twink's height came forward, with bright crimson hair and white wings. He stood with his nose in the air, not looking at her.

'Perfect!' exclaimed Maximus, clasping his hands together. 'You two will be partners in the Friendship Dance. Now, who's next?' he continued. 'Miss Wintersong, please step forward . . .'

Twink stood uncertainly in place while Maximus decided on the other partners. Snow ended up with the first boy, and gave a little skip of delight. Twink rolled her eyes. She supposed he had been the 'swoony' one!

While Maximus dithered over the final two pairs, Twink glanced at her own partner. She supposed she might as well be friendly, if they were going to be stuck together for the next two weeks.

'Hi, I'm Twink,' she whispered. 'What's your name?'

Slowly, the boy turned to face her. His lip curled as though he smelled something bad. 'Why do you want to know?' he drawled.

'Why?' Twink gaped at him. 'Well – we can't call each other "Miss" and "Master" for two whole weeks, can we?'

The boy sniffed. *Why ever not?* his expression seemed to say. 'I'm Chauncey-Oberon,' he said finally. 'And I'm actually Master Sparkworth the *Third*, if you must know.'

Chauncey-Oberon? What a funny, stuck-up name! 'But your friends don't call you that, do they?' ventured Twink. 'Don't you have a nickname?'

The boy glared at her. His school uniform included a long purple cape, and he swept it importantly over one arm. 'As I *said*, I'm called Chauncey-Oberon. What's wrong with that?'

'Nothing,' said Twink, taken aback. 'It's just – well, it's such a long name, so I thought –'

'What of it?' demanded the boy. 'Is Twink *all* you're called? How common!' He turned away, spreading his wings wide to block Twink out.

Twink's fists clenched as hot anger swept over her. What an awful boy! And she actually had to dance a *friendship* dance with him?

She was still seething as Maximus formed the four partners into a square. 'We shall learn the first steps today,' he announced. 'Everyone hold hands.'

Gritting her teeth, Twink held Chauncey-Oberon's hand as lightly as possible. At least he looked as revolted as she did.

The portly fairy was surprisingly graceful as he demonstrated a series of moves. 'Girls to the left . . . boys to the right . . . now turn!' The footwork was tricky, and Twink had to concentrate to master it – a

task made all the more difficult by Chauncey-Oberon's sneers.

'*Do* be careful,' he hissed when she trod on his toes by mistake. Twink scowled. Next time, she'd stomp as hard as she could!

An hour later, Twink's head was whirling with new steps. She was relieved when Maximus finally clapped his hands, signalling for them to stop.

'We'll begin again tomorrow morning, nine o'clock sharp,' he said. 'Now, follow the butterflies to your rooms – you have half an hour to freshen up before dinner. Make *sure* you all look presentable!'

He gazed sternly at them, and then flitted away under a leafy arch. A pair of butterflies appeared – one bright blue, the other red. They bobbed in front of the young fairies.

Jena laughed. 'I suppose blue is for sapphire. Are you boys in Ruby Room, by any chance?'

'How did you guess?' grinned her partner, an older fairy called Palo.

Twink lagged glumly behind as the little crowd fluttered off after the butterflies. 'What school are you from?' she heard Tilli's partner ask her. He sounded polite and interested. In fact, all three of the other boys seemed nice.

It's just me who has the awful one, thought Twink. Imagine two whole weeks with Chauncey-Oberon! Even now he wasn't looking at her, but flew with his nose in the air, gazing straight ahead.

Snow's partner – who Twink had learned was really called Gem, instead of Master Greenbranch – gave him a friendly nudge. 'You all right there, Chaunce?'

'Chauncey-Oberon,' corrected Twink's partner coldly, sweeping his cape about himself. 'I did tell you earlier, but I suppose it was too difficult.'

Gem rolled his eyes. 'Well, I only go to Windy Hill, you know – not White Cloud, like *some* fairies.' He and the other boys exchanged a grimace. Obviously, realised Twink, they didn't like Chauncey-Oberon much either!

About midway down the bush, the butterflies fluttered off in different directions. 'See you at dinner,' called Jena after the boys. 'Make sure you're *presentable*!'

The moment the boys were out of earshot, Snow gave an excited bounce. 'Ooh! Do you think he likes me?'

'Who?' asked Jena, inspecting herself in her little mirror again. Watching her curiously, Twink thought it seemed like just a habit, rather than being vain.

'*Gem*, that's who!' groaned Tilli as they flitted around a branch. 'No, I don't think he likes you, Snow – or at least not *that* way. We're all too young for that.'

'You don't?' said Snow in surprise. 'But . . . he held my hand, and –'

'Everyone was holding someone's hand,' said Jena, snapping her mirror shut again. 'Don't be silly, Snow. It was just part of the dance, that's all.' Snow fell silent, looking crestfallen.

The blue butterfly swooped to a halt in front of Sapphire Room. 'Thanks,' said Jena as they entered the glittering chamber. 'Could you come back when it's time for dinner?' The butterfly dipped a wing at her, and floated off through the branches.

Trying to lighten the mood as they changed out of their school uniforms, Twink said, 'Anyway, I'm positive Chauncey-Oberon doesn't like *me*. He probably wishes the sparkle-seeker had chosen any other fairy at Glitterwings!'

Tilli grinned as she combed her bright yellow hair. 'Yes, you really drew the short grass with old C-O, didn't you?' She pulled a haughty face. 'That's *Chauncey-Oberon* to you lot!'

Twink and Snow burst out laughing. Tilli imitated the stuck-up fairy perfectly!

'Yes, I wonder what the story is there?' said Jena thoughtfully.

'What do you mean?' asked Snow. 'He's not a story, he's a nightmare – and poor Twink has to dance with him!'

Jena shrugged, giving her wings a quick polish. 'Yes, but fairies who are so unpleasant usually aren't very happy themselves. So I just wonder what's made him that way, that's all.'

'Who cares?' said Tilli, pulling a ruffly carnation-petal dress over her head. 'Plenty of fairies have

42

problems – that doesn't make it all right to act like a puffed-up toad!'

All of the girls' parents had made sure that their daughters had a pretty dress to wear for the evenings. Twink's own parents had sent her very nicest rose-petal dress. She tied the sash around her waist, deep in thought.

On the whole, she agreed with Tilli: even if Chauncey-Oberon was unhappy, that didn't mean he could treat other fairies however he pleased.

Was he unhappy, though? Twink frowned. He

didn't act like it – he just seemed full of himself, and very, very rude! Still, she found herself wondering if there was perhaps more to Chauncey-Oberon than she'd first thought.

I'll keep trying to be nice to him, Twink decided, putting on her favourite necklace – a tiny daisy on a woven chain. *It can't hurt – and I'll feel better about myself if I'm not as awful as he is.*

'Look, the butterfly's back already,' said Jena. 'Come on, we'd better hurry!'

The girls followed the bright blue insect as it led them upwards again. Twink was struck suddenly by how attractive the four of them looked – all in their best dresses, with hair and wings gleaming. It was as if they belonged in this grand place!

She had forgotten all about the shadowy figure that had been peering at her earlier . . . but it hadn't forgotten her. Something was crouched behind a large green leaf, watching her every move.

Chapter Four

The blue butterfly led them to a large, ornate tree house. Adult fairies were swooping through the carved double doors, paying no attention to them. They all wore the finest orchids and lilies, and bright gemstones flashed everywhere.

Twink gulped. Had she really thought that she and the others looked as if they belonged here? Compared to these fairies, they should be doing the cleaning!

The boys were there already, and seemed just as uncertain as they did. Gem peeked through the

door, and his face paled. 'It's all adults, sitting at a big long table. I think it's the Queen's counsellors – we *can't* be meant to be eating with them!'

Maximus appeared beside them, flapping his wings irritably. 'Children! I *did* ask you to be prompt – that doesn't mean hanging about like hooligans. Come along, now.'

Maximus herded the eight of them inside. Twink caught her breath. The high, arched hall was made almost entirely of windows, showing leaves and branches all around them. As Gem had said, a long table ran down the length of it with dozens of adult fairies already seated.

'You're down here, at the bottom of the table,' said Maximus, guiding them to their places.

Instead of the friendly spotted mushrooms that Twink was used to at Glitterwings, the palace seats were carved from wood, each made to look like a different woodland animal. Twink's was a frog with glistening emerald eyes. She sat on it gingerly, half expecting it to say *ribbit*!

Chauncey-Oberon had seemed as daunted as the

rest of them before, but now he surveyed his surroundings with a condescending look. 'Not bad, I suppose,' he said once Maximus had bustled off. 'Of course, this is only the Queen's *summer* palace.'

'And of course *you* know all about it,' snapped Palo. From the sharpness of his tone, Twink guessed that Chauncey-Oberon hadn't been endearing himself to the other boys since they'd seen them last!

'I do actually,' said Chauncey-Oberon, stretching his wings. 'My parents are *very* important, you know. In fact, the Queen knows me personally. I'm sure that's why I was chosen for the dance.'

'I doubt it's anything to do with that,' said Jena mildly. 'It's a magical dance, that's all – it needs certain fairies.'

Chauncey-Oberon sniffed. It was clear from his haughty expression that he thought he knew far more about it than Jena.

Twink gritted her teeth. He was even worse than before! Still, remembering that she'd planned to be nice to him, she forced a smile. 'What's White Cloud like, Chauncey-Oberon?' she asked.

He raised his crimson eyebrows, as if he couldn't believe Twink was daring to talk to him. 'Very nice,' he said, sneering at her down his long nose. 'We don't get *common* fairies there.'

'No, just moss brains like you,' muttered Tilli's partner, a slightly chubby fairy called Jay.

Twink glared at Chauncey-Oberon, her resolve forgotten. 'Why do you keep going on about fairies being common?' she demanded. 'My father says it doesn't matter how old someone's family is, or who they know – it's how they act that counts!'

'Well, he *would* say that, wouldn't he?' said Chauncey-Oberon, stifling a yawn. 'After all, *he's* not anyone important.'

Oh! Twink's blood sizzled in her veins. But before she could say anything else, a rustling noise filled the long room. All of the fairies rose from their seats, standing respectfully on tiptoe.

'*The Queen!*' squeaked Snow, turning as pale as her hair.

Twink's heart thundered as she and the others leapt up. It had never occurred to her that they might see Queen Mab before the day of the celebrations.

A pair of songbirds stood one on either side of the doors, trilling a bright fountain of notes. There was an expectant silence . . . and then Queen Mab fluttered in, with four attendants behind her.

Twink let out a breath. The Queen was just as beautiful as she remembered, with long, flowing golden hair and a silvery dress gleaming with moonstones.

Queen Mab's gaze fell on the young fairies, and a smile lit her face. 'You must be the dancers,' she said warmly, pausing beside them. 'Thank you very much for coming from your schools to wish me a happy birthday.'

'You're welcome, Your Majesty,' murmured Twink with the others. Although she knew Queen Mab had lived for several centuries, the fairy monarch seemed to glow with ageless beauty. Twink's wings tingled to be so close to her.

'And Twink! How lovely to see you again, my dear. I'm so glad you were one of the ones chosen.'

Stooping, the Queen kissed Twink's cheek lightly before continuing down the room.

The other young fairies gaped at her. Jena recovered first, gazing at Chauncey-Oberon with an amused smile. Twink thought he looked like the carved frog on her chair, all goggling eyes and open mouth!

Far away at the head of the table, the Queen took her seat, gracefully spreading open her golden wings behind her. 'Please be seated,' she said.

The hall filled with noise as everyone sat down and began talking. Tilli lunged across the table towards Twink. 'What was that?' she hissed excitedly. 'How do you know the Queen? You never said!'

Twink's cheeks reddened as the others leaned towards her as well, their faces alight with curiosity – except for Chauncey-Oberon, who looked extremely cross.

'It's nothing, really,' she said. 'Our school hosted the ice pole a couple of winters ago, and I met her then.'

The fairies exchanged a doubtful glance. 'Twink, she came to *our* school last year too, and she didn't know me from a bump on a log,' pointed out Jay.

'Yes, I think there must be more to it than that!' laughed Jena. 'Come on, Twink, tell us.' A rainbow of butterflies streamed into the hall, carrying seed cakes and nectar on gleaming mother-of-pearl trays.

Twink hesitated. Should she should tell them about Stripe, the wasp she'd befriended during her first year at Glitterwings? Queen Mab had been so impressed when she heard that she'd wanted to meet Twink, and had decided to make friends with the wasps herself.

But the Queen's attempt to befriend the wasps hadn't gone very well. In fact, Twink's father had told her just a few days ago that things were worse than ever between the two species.

'It's no one's fault,' he'd said sadly. 'But wasps and fairies are very different, you know, Twinkster. There was another meeting recently between Queen Mab and the wasp Queen, and somehow it all went wrong. They just couldn't understand each other's point of view.'

The news had distressed Twink a great deal. She hated to think of fairies and wasps not getting on, when she and Stripe had been so close. But it was just how things were. A lot of fairies couldn't stand the very *mention* of wasps!

What if . . . what if her new friends felt the same way? Twink's wings chilled at the thought.

The others were still waiting for her to answer. Twink forced a smile. 'Honestly, that's all there is to it. Queen Mab liked how I danced in the ice pole dance, and so we chatted for a bit afterwards. That's all.'

Chauncey-Oberon's face was red. 'So I suppose *that's* why you were chosen for the Friendship Dance!' he burst out. 'Because the Queen felt sorry for you.'

Thoughts of wasps flew from Twink's head. 'Felt *sorry* for me? But I never said –'

'Well, what else could it have been?' demanded Chauncey-Oberon. 'There's no other reason why she might talk to an ordinary fairy like *you*. Why,

I've never even heard of your parents! I bet they –'

'I think that's enough,' broke in Gem angrily.

The crimson-haired fairy stumbled to a halt, looking surprised.

'Yes, *I'll* say it is,' agreed Palo. 'Listen, Chauncey-Oberon. We boys have to live with you for the next two weeks, so it had better be understood right now that you're going to behave yourself.'

Chauncey-Oberon curled his lip. 'Oh? What's *that* supposed to mean?'

Palo gripped the shoulder of the younger fairy's purple cloak and pulled him towards him. 'It means that from now on, you're going to *keep your mouth shut*. If I hear you say anything I don't like, you WILL regret it. Understood?'

Chauncey-Oberon paled. 'Er . . .'

'Yes, and that goes for us girls as well,' put in Jena. 'We won't have you being horrid, not to Twink or any of the rest of us, so you might as well stop it right now!' The little fairy's eyes flashed.

Chauncey-Oberon tried to sneer, but Twink thought he seemed worried. 'Whatever,' he

muttered. 'As if I'd want to talk to *you* lot, anyway!'

He was silent for the rest of the meal, glaring down at his food as the rest of them swapped stories about their schools. Tilli soon had them all laughing loudly about Emerald Leaf, but Chauncey-Oberon didn't even look up.

Though he'd brought it on himself, Twink couldn't help feeling a bit sorry for the crimson-haired fairy – it couldn't be nice to have everyone turn on you, when you'd only just met them!

And besides . . . would the others still have stuck up for her, if they'd known the truth about how she met the Queen? The thought prickled at Twink uncomfortably.

After dessert, Maximus bustled over to them. 'You may take your leave now, children,' he said. 'Rise, and bow to the Queen.'

They did so. Twink's pointed ears grew warm as she saw the entire room smiling indulgently at them. 'Our dancers!' called Queen Mab, and everyone burst into polite applause, beating their wings together.

'I hope they're still applauding *after* they see us dance,' muttered Tilli, pink-cheeked.

As they flew from the room, Twink found herself next to Chauncey-Oberon. She cleared her throat. 'Listen,' she started, 'I'm sorry about –'

He glared at her. 'Oh, just leave me alone!' he snapped. And before Twink could respond, he had jetted off after the other boys.

Chapter
Five

The two weeks passed in a whirlwind of dance lessons and new experiences. Before Twink knew it, it was the day before the Queen's birthday.

'And turn, arms up,' instructed Maximus as he took them through one of their last practices. 'We're nearing the final quadrille . . . flower steps please, *slowly* . . . watch your feet, Master Greenbranch!'

Though Twink tried her best to concentrate, it wasn't easy. All around them, the courtyard was being turned into a glittering wonderland for the Queen's birthday. Everywhere Twink looked, there

were strings of bright, shining crystals, and long garlands of white and yellow flowers.

If only she didn't have to worry about their dance! Though she knew the Friendship Dance backwards and forwards now, the thought of performing it in front of hundreds of fairies made Twink's wings turn cold.

It was such a funny, old-fashioned dance, too. There were lots of flutterings and little hops in it, but the fairies never took to the air. And, unlike a lot of magical dances, they didn't have to focus their mind on anything in particular.

Which was a good thing, thought Twink as she bobbed and spun with the others. If the Friendship Dance had required them to really feel friendship towards their partners, she'd have been in trouble!

For, despite Palo and Jena's threats on their first day, Chauncey-Oberon obviously hated Twink, and muttered snide remarks at her whenever he could. '*Commoner*' was his favourite, always said in a sneering tone.

Twink thought about telling Jena or Palo, but

didn't really want to make a fuss. They were only at the palace for a short while – surely she could ignore him for that long!

Besides, the other fairies more than made up for Chauncey-Oberon's unpleasantness. The three girls especially – they'd had some glimmery times in Sapphire Room over the last two weeks. Twink smiled, remembering a flying pillow fight just the night before.

'We're almost at the finish,' called Maximus. 'Hold that pose . . . and gentlemen bow, ladies curtsy!'

Out of breath from the long dance, Twink dipped into a curtsy, holding her lavender wings gracefully behind her back. Chauncey-Oberon bowed stiffly from the waist, not looking at her.

'Excellent!' exclaimed Maximus, his chubby face beaming. 'You should all do very well at the party tomorrow. Now, your outfits need a final fitting, so –'

'Can I ask a question?' broke in Snow, raising her hand.

Maximus blinked in surprise. 'Certainly, Miss Wintersong.'

'Well – I know the Friendship Dance is magical, but . . . what does it actually do?' Snow's pale cheeks reddened. 'I mean – how will we know whether it's working or not?'

Twink nodded as the others murmured in agreement. It was something they had all wondered.

Maximus shook his head. 'My dear Miss Wintersong, the Friendship Dance is very powerful, very old magic. It is not like some of your modern dances, all flash and sparkle! Its spell wraps subtly around an audience. It enhances their own friendships, and heals where there have been problems.'

Twink and Tilli exchanged a confused glance. What did *that* mean?

Snow's white eyebrows creased. 'But . . . well, what I mean is, I don't *feel* it. With most dances, you feel the magic happening, even when you're practising. This one just feels like we're doing ordinary steps.'

'No, one often doesn't feel the Friendship Dance

when one's doing it – not until the time is right,' allowed Maximus. 'As I said, it is very old magic, and it works in deep ways.'

A pair of workers flew past, carrying a daisy in a carved walnut-shell pot. 'Why does it matter who dances it?' asked Palo with a frown. 'I know we were all chosen for a reason, but *what* reason?'

Maximus drew himself up to his full, diminutive height. 'The Dance does the choosing. It is not for us to question it.'

'Funny sort of dance for a birthday, anyway,' muttered Chauncey-Oberon. '*I'd* rather have the Felicitations Dance, if it were me.'

Though his tone was as rude as ever, Twink thought he had a point. The Felicitations Dance was such a bright, cheerful dance, and was traditional at fairy birthday celebrations. Compared to it, the Friendship Dance was so slow it was almost boring.

Maximus's face turned berry-red. 'For your information, Master Sparkworth, the *Queen* herself requested this dance, and that it be performed by schoolchildren! Now away with you – it's time for your final fittings.' He flitted off, his robes flapping behind him.

'Oh, well done, moss brain,' said Gem to Chauncey-Oberon. 'Maximus is really cross with us now!' The crimson-haired fairy scowled, and didn't answer.

'It's interesting that the Queen requested the dance, though,' said Jena as the blue and red butterflies fluttered towards them. 'I wonder why?'

The fairies flew after their butterfly guides, talking about what Maximus had said. On impulse, Twink lagged behind, gazing up at the Queen's residence. She had been curious about it ever since she first saw it – what was it like inside?

Suddenly she gasped in surprise. There was Queen Mab herself, looking down at the courtyard from a palace window! *Why, she looks sad,* thought Twink in amazement.

The thought startled her. She had never thought of the Queen as a fairy who might have ordinary feelings. But why should she feel unhappy, seeing all of her sparkling birthday decorations?

Twink had no idea, but there was no mistaking the Queen's expression. Sympathy rushed over her. Whatever the problem was, she wished with all her heart that she could do something to help.

Queen Mab saw her then. Twink gulped as their eyes met. She had found out very quickly that there were a lot of rules in the palace – had she somehow broken one by watching the Queen?

But Queen Mab only gave her a small, sad smile, and turned away.

The four girls stood in Sapphire Room as the palace dressmaker, Miss Organdy, bustled about with her assistants.

'Very nice,' said Miss Organdy, making an adjustment to Twink's bow. 'Now, don't you dare eat too much dinner tonight, young lady – that dress is going to fit perfectly, if I have anything to do with it!'

Twink gazed at herself in the mirror in wonder. Her dress was made from pure white orchid cloth, and glittered with seed pearls and tiny emeralds. She had never dreamed she could look so pretty!

Miss Organdy turned to the other girls then. Changing her clothes, Twink drifted to the window. The sun was just setting, and the leaves and branches seemed to glow with a golden light. The palace tree houses nestled on their perches, each one fantastical and different.

Propping her elbows on the sill, Twink gazed at her favourite: a small, cosy-looking house with a round turret and jewelled carvings of butterflies. She

loved imagining that it belonged to Bimi and her, and that she and her best friend could wake up every morning in this magical place!

'It's really glimmery here, isn't it?' said a voice beside her. Twink glanced up as Tilli sat on the sill beside her.

Twink nodded. 'It's even more beautiful than Glitterwings. But I'll still be glad to get back to school again.' She smiled at the thought of seeing Bimi and the others. What a lot she'd have to tell them!

'Really?' said Tilli in surprise. 'Wasps, I'm dreading it! But then, you *like* your school,' she added glumly. 'I suppose it makes a difference.'

Twink nudged Tilli's wing with her own. 'Tilli, why *don't* you change schools? Come to Glitterwings! You'd love it there.'

Tilli heaved a sigh. 'Oh, I don't know. Maybe I'll talk to my mum. Anyway, Twink, let's stay in touch, all right? Your family's house isn't far from mine – it would be great to get together over the hols.'

'Yes, I'd love to!' exclaimed Twink. The sunny-

haired fairy was her favourite of the three girls, and they'd had a lot of fun together over the last two weeks.

'Great, *that's* settled, then,' grinned Tilli. 'At least it gives me something to look forward to at awful old Emerald Leaf! Oh, look,' she added, peering out of the window. 'There's our good friend, C-O, as cheerful as ever.'

Following Tilli's gaze, Twink saw Chauncey-Oberon sitting on a branch by himself. He had his knees pulled up to his chest, and as usual there was a scowl on his face.

The sight of him made Twink feel cross herself. 'What's *wrong* with him?' she burst out. 'He acts like he hates everything!'

Tilli glanced over her shoulder at Miss Organdy and her helpers, still busy with Snow and Jena.

'You know how he's always going on about how important his family is?' she whispered. 'Well, Jay said it's really true; his parents are both ambassadors for the Queen. But he never sees them, because they spend all their time travelling. He was brought up by nurses, in a big empty house.'

Twink's anger faded. 'Really? But – that's terrible.' She couldn't imagine never seeing her parents; how awful! Even worse would be the knowledge that they thought their job was more important than she was. 'Do you think that's why he hates everything?' she asked.

Tilli shrugged. 'It wouldn't make *me* very happy. But I still don't think he should go around acting like he's got a nettle under his wing – he just makes everything worse for himself.'

Twink watched as the crimson-haired boy flew

sullenly away towards the boys' tree house. 'How does Jay know?' she asked. She couldn't imagine Chauncey-Oberon actually *telling* anyone all that!

'He has a friend at White Cloud,' said Tilli. 'He and the other boys wanted to tease C-O, so Jay wrote and asked his friend what he knew about Chauncey-Oberon. But when he found out, they decided not to say anything after all. It would have been pretty mean, I suppose.'

Twink nodded. Despite Chauncey-Oberon's nasty comments to her, she was very glad that the others hadn't used their knowledge about his family to taunt him. Nobody deserved that, not even him.

'What's so fascinating out there?' asked Snow, flinging herself chummily between them. 'Ooh look, it's sunset – how pretty!'

Exchanging a look, Twink and Tilli agreed silently not to tell Snow. They both liked the pretty, white-haired fairy, but she *did* tend to blurt things out sometimes – it would be terrible if she told Chauncey-Oberon what they knew!

Miss Organdy and her helpers were just leaving,

carrying the girls' dresses with them – each carefully wrapped in rose petals. Jena yawned, stretching her wings. 'What a palaver, eh?' she said cheerfully. 'Come on, you lot, we'd better get ready for dinner. Isn't it strange, how we're always having to change our clothes here?'

'Oh, palace life!' cried Snow, twirling away from the window and fluttering her wings dramatically. 'It's just too difficult!'

Everyone laughed. With an inward grin, Twink thought how funny it was that Snow's crush on Gem had all but vanished as she got to know him. Now it was one of the Queen's young counsellors who she thought was 'swoony', and they all teased her mercilessly!

After one last look at the sunset – now blazing rosy-orange behind the leaves – Twink started to turn from the window. All at once a prickling sensation ran across her wings, as if she were being watched. Looking back again, she gasped.

There was a pair of large, dark eyes, peering out at her from behind a nearby leaf.

Chapter Six

Twink stared back at the eyes, her heart thudding as she remembered the shadowy face that she'd seen on her first day here.

Since then, she'd often had the uncomfortable feeling that she was being observed by someone, but had thought it was only her imagination. Yet there was nothing made-up about the eyes watching her now.

In fact . . . Twink leaned out of the window to get a closer look. It was almost as if the eyes were *asking* her something. There was an imploring expression

in them, as though whoever it was needed Twink's help in some way . . .

She started as Tilli reappeared. 'Twink, what's up?'

'Look!' Twink clutched her arm and pointed. 'Do you see it?'

'See what?' asked Tilli blankly. And suddenly Twink realised that the eyes were gone.

'I –' Her ears went hot as she gazed at the place where the eyes had been. She'd sound like an idiot if she tried to explain! 'Never mind,' she said finally. 'Come on, let's get ready for dinner.'

The Queen's birthday dawned bright and sunny, with a sharp autumn tang to the air.

Twink and the others practised the Friendship Dance for the final time that morning – earning a 'Bravo!' from Maximus – before hastily returning to their rooms to get changed. The party would begin soon, though their dance wasn't scheduled until later that afternoon. Twink wished glumly that they could just get it over with, so she could enjoy herself!

Sapphire Room was full of bustling attendants helping the girls to get ready. 'This is silly!' laughed Jena. 'We're perfectly capable of doing it ourselves.' But clearly no one agreed with her.

Twink sat very still as a pretty attendant with yellow wings did her hair, and another brushed diamond dust on to her wings. *Diamond dust!* Twink felt unreal, as if she were living a story in a petal mag. When they finally eased the orchid frock over her head, Twink stared at her own reflection. She couldn't speak.

Her dress looked even lovelier than before – and so did she. Her long pink hair was caught elegantly back at the sides with emerald combs, and her wings sparkled like sun on morning dew.

'Oh, aren't we beautiful!' breathed Snow. Ruby combs gleamed in her hair.

Tilli shook her head in a daze. 'I hardly know myself.'

'Well, it's still just us,' said Jena. 'But we *do* look nice, don't we?' She inspected herself in her little mirror with satisfaction.

Secretly, Twink thought that Jena looked the prettiest of them all. As the oldest, her long hair was arranged on top of her head, with little purple tendrils escaping down. Her dress was decorated with real diamonds that sparkled in the sun.

Jena snapped her mirror shut. 'Are we ready, then?'

Twink's stomach lurched in alarm. 'But – it's still ages until our dance, isn't it?'

One of the attendants laughed. 'Yes, but you're to be in the courtyard as soon as you're ready. The party's about to begin!'

With the blue butterfly leading the way, the girls flew slowly towards the top of the palace, taking care not to crease their dresses. Everyone they passed smiled and nodded at them, and despite her nervousness, Twink couldn't help feeling very grand.

Suddenly she remembered how Bimi had got so carried away during their second-year fashion show, and she had to laugh at herself. *I'd better not get too used to this*, thought Twink as they landed in the courtyard. *It's back to real life tomorrow!*

The courtyard was already a-flutter with fairies, all as richly dressed as the girls. Long tables of mouth-watering food had been set out, and a cricket band was playing a light, lilting tune.

The boys appeared, looking stiff and uncomfortable in their formal clothes. 'Did you ever see anything so silly?' said Gem glumly, gazing down at his jewel-encrusted tunic. 'How do the palace fairies ever play Fledge, or – or fly at high speed, or –'

'Oh, stop it!' laughed Jena. 'It's just for one day. I think you all look really nice.'

The boys scowled, though Twink thought they looked rather pleased as well. All except Chauncey-Oberon, of course. The crimson-haired fairy stood on his own, surveying the glittering courtyard with a haughty expression.

Twink was startled to see that his tunic and trousers were white with emeralds, like hers. Her cheeks flared. Though she felt sorry for Chauncey-Oberon after what Tilli had told her, she still didn't want to wear matching clothes with him!

The courtyard buzzed with activity as more and more fairies arrived, each looking grander and more important than the last. Waiters flitted through the crowd, carrying trays laden with delicate seed cakes.

Had the Queen made an appearance yet? Twink stood on tiptoe, craning to see.

'Tilli, have you –' she started, and then stopped as she realised that Tilli was nowhere to be seen. Nor were any of the others – she'd somehow got separated from them in the crowd.

Frowning anxiously, Twink looked all around her, but she was completely hemmed in by brightly coloured wings and flashing jewels. Too shy to draw attention to herself by taking to the air, Twink withdrew to the edge of the courtyard and perched carefully on the smooth wooden railing.

If I just sit still, one of them will find me, she told herself. And meanwhile, she had a glimmery view of what had to be the most sumptuous party ever!

But she didn't get to enjoy it for very long. A moment later there was a soft scrabbling noise in the branches behind her – and that prickling sensation across her wings again! Turning quickly, Twink's violet eyes widened.

'*Stripe!*' she gasped. The black and yellow insect clinging to a nearby branch was larger than the wasp Twink had known, but it was really him, there was no mistaking it!

Twink's heart leapt. Without thinking, she flitted over the railing and gave Stripe a joyful hug. He felt as soft as she remembered! Stripe buzzed happily, clearly just as glad to see her.

But this was no good – they'd be seen by someone

at the party. 'Come on,' whispered Twink. 'Let's go back into the branches a bit.'

Soon she and Stripe were sitting on a branch deep in the bush, with the noise of the party behind them. 'Are *you* the one who's been watching me?' demanded Twink. 'But Stripe, why didn't you just come out and say hello?'

Stripe shook his head, pointing back at the party. His large eyes looked sad.

'No, I – I suppose that wouldn't have been a good idea, would it?' said Twink slowly, her heart heavy. 'My father says things are worse than ever between the wasps and the fairies now. You had to wait until you were sure you wouldn't be seen, didn't you?'

Stripe nodded. Though wasps couldn't talk as fairies did, Twink and Stripe had always communicated easily, and now was no exception.

With a mix of expressive buzzes and acting things out, Stripe quickly explained that he and his parents had moved to a nest near here, soon after he'd said goodbye to Twink for the last time.

He had thought he'd never see her again – but

then two weeks ago, he had been amazed to spot Twink arriving at the fairy palace on a hawk! Longing to speak to his friend once more, Stripe had been trying to get Twink on her own ever since she first arrived.

But now . . . Stripe seemed to falter. He shook his head, looking worried.

'What is it?' cried Twink. 'Oh, Stripe, something's happened, hasn't it?'

In answer, the wasp slumped down weakly, making his wings go limp and lolling his head to one side. Before Twink could react, he had sat up again, looking at her with imploring eyes.

'Someone's ill!' exclaimed Twink. Stripe nodded. Taking the hem of Twink's dress in his mouth, he lifted into the air, tugging urgently at it.

Twink gasped as she realised what he meant. 'You want *me* to go? But Stripe, I can't! It's the Queen's party!'

Stripe stared at her in dismay. Guilt pierced Twink. 'And – and besides, Stripe, I'm still only a student. If someone's really hurt, what could *I* do?'

You helped me *when* I *was injured*, said Stripe's expression.

'Yes, but . . .' Twink swallowed hard. 'Stripe, is it really urgent? It can't wait for even a few hours?'

The wasp's buzz clearly meant, *No, it can't!*

Twink rubbed her wings together worriedly. Glancing back towards the party, she could just glimpse the fine clothes and flashing wings through the leaves.

How could she think of leaving? Queen Mab herself had asked for the magical Friendship Dance! If she left now, and she wasn't back in time . . . Twink gulped. She didn't even want to imagine it!

But how could she say no to Stripe? One of his friends must be very ill – possibly even dying. Though Twink didn't have as much knowledge as a Fairy Medic, she did know *some* things. She might be able to help. And their dance wasn't due to begin for several more hours.

'All right!' she decided quickly, hardly able to believe what she was saying. 'I've got a box of fairy dust back in our room – I'll just swoop by and get it, and then we can go –'

'Go where?' asked a suspicious voice.

Whirling round, Twink saw Chauncey-Oberon hovering just a few branches away. His jaw slackened as he caught sight of Stripe. 'That's a *wasp*!' he burst out.

'So what?' retorted Twink – though she didn't feel nearly as defiant as she sounded. What if Chauncey-Oberon went back to the party and told everyone?

Instead the crimson-haired fairy flitted forward, staring at Stripe. The wasp buzzed warningly as he got too close, and Chauncey-Oberon darted back. 'What's he doing here?' he demanded.

'He's got a hurt friend,' said Twink shortly. 'He wants me to go and help.'

Chauncey-Oberon frowned. '*You? Why?*'

'I –' Heat swept up Twink's neck. 'Because – because I helped him before,' she admitted, her cheeks on fire.

Realisation dawned across Chauncey-Oberon's face. 'Hang on, you're *that* Glitterwings student! We heard at White Cloud that one of them had made friends with a wasp. That was *you*, wasn't it?'

'Yes,' said Twink, shifting uncomfortably. Why was he staring at her like that?

'So that's how you know the Queen,' murmured Chauncey-Oberon, looking at Stripe again. 'I heard she was really impressed by it – she tried to make friends with the wasps for ages afterwards, didn't she? She and the wasp Queen had a meeting just a few weeks ago, but it didn't work out.'

'That's right.' Twink glanced anxiously at the sun. She didn't have time for this! 'Listen, Chauncey-Oberon, I have to go now. If I hurry, I should be back in time for the dance, but –'

His eyes narrowed. 'Oh, no you don't! You thought you'd sneak off and be a big hero again, didn't you? Well, I don't think so!'

Twink stared at him. 'What are you talking about?'

'It's obvious!' cried Chauncey-Oberon, his face reddening. 'The Queen was impressed *last* time when you helped a wasp, so now you want to do it again and upstage the rest of us – get all the glory for yourself!'

Twink's mouth fell open as Stripe buzzed angrily at her side. 'Are you mad?' she spluttered. 'I do not! Stripe's my friend and he needs help, that's all.'

'Well, I won't let you,' went on Chauncey-Oberon as if she hadn't spoken. His fists clenched. 'If anyone deserves to impress the Queen, it's *me*, not you! I'm coming with you.'

'*What?*' shrieked Twink. She clapped her hand

over her mouth, glancing back through the leaves at the party. 'You are not!' she hissed.

Chauncey-Oberon folded his arms across his chest. 'Try and stop me! I'll go straight to Maximus if you do – and you know *he'd* never let you leave the party now, no matter what!'

Twink gritted her teeth. Oh, how she wished she could tell this awful boy to just flap off! But she knew Chauncey-Oberon would do exactly as he said if she didn't give in.

'Face it, Twink, I've outsmarted you,' he said smugly. 'If *you* get to be a hero, then I'm going to be one too – and that's all there is to it.'

'Come on, then,' snapped Twink. 'We have to hurry. But I'm warning you, Chauncey-Oberon – if you don't actually *help* me with this injured wasp, then – then Stripe will sting you!'

Chapter Seven

'Is this the place?' whispered Twink, gazing at the hollow tree. After they had sneaked out of the palace, Stripe had led them deep into the wood. Now he nodded, motioning for them to hurry.

Twink started to fly forward, clutching the little box of fairy dust she'd brought from her room – and then squawked in surprise as Chauncey-Oberon jerked her back.

'That's a *nest*!' he hissed.

Twink's throat went dry as she saw that he was right: the hollow tree had a steady stream of wasps

flying in and out of it. She felt cold suddenly. She hadn't reckoned on actually going inside a wasps' nest!

Stripe tugged at her orchid dress again, his eyes begging her to continue. Twink took a deep breath. 'All right, Stripe – I'm coming.'

'*What?*' yelped Chauncey-Oberon. 'But we can't go in there!'

'*I* am,' snapped Twink, shaking him off. 'If you want to stay behind, that's fine with me – I wish you would!'

Twink sped after Stripe. Reluctantly, Chauncey-Oberon followed. His complexion had gone a bit green, Twink noticed coldly. Apparently being a hero wasn't quite what he'd expected!

But even Twink gulped as they landed on the hollow tree's rim, high over the ground. From here, the hole into the tree looked like a gaping cavern. She could hear the low drone of hundreds of wasps buzzing inside.

Suddenly a pair of the insects flew out. Twink leapt back with a startled squeak, almost dropping

the fairy dust. The wasps reared back also, looking just as alarmed as she felt.

But then they caught sight of Stripe, and their expressions changed. With a respectful nod, they flew on, buzzing off into the distance.

'What was *that* about?' asked Twink in confusion.

Stripe looked embarrassed. Pointing first at her and then himself, he mimed a very important-looking wasp – and then shrugged sheepishly.

'You mean you're famous?' gasped Twink. 'Because of me?'

'That means *you're* famous too, in the wasp world,' put in Chauncey-Oberon nastily. 'How sweet!'

Stripe frowned at his tone of voice. *Never mind that now!* his expression said.

Beckoning for them to follow, he flew into the hollow tree. The two fairies followed after him. Twink had expected utter darkness, but to her surprise there were little holes in the wood that let in light – almost like the windows at Glitterwings.

Stripe led them to a door set in a smooth paper

wall that stretched across the inside of the tree. Twink gasped as they passed through the doorway. They were in a six-sided corridor, made of a sturdy white paper that seemed to gleam with a light of its own.

The passageway was too low for the fairies to fly in, and they had to walk hunched over as Stripe led them through a maze of corridors. Twink's legs and wings were soon aching from the unnatural position.

The buzzing noise roared in their ears. A constant stream of wasps flitted past, looking amazed to see them. Twink smiled weakly as she passed an elderly wasp. His eyes bulged, and he flew away in alarm.

'I think we're in their palace!' exclaimed Chauncey-Oberon. He pointed to the walls. They were covered in murals – and for the first time, Twink noticed that they all showed a wasp wearing a crown.

'Excellent!' said Chauncey-Oberon smugly. 'It'll be even more impressive if we help a really *important* wasp.'

Twink glared at him – but all the same, a dreadful thought occurred to her. 'Chauncey-Oberon, you don't think – I mean, it *can't* be the Queen who –'

Stripe darted back, buzzing anxiously. Grasping Twink's hem, he dragged them forward. They came to a low door, guarded by a pair of sentries who flew aside for them.

Entering the hexagonal chamber, Twink saw that

her fears were right. The wasp that lay on the high paper bed was very poorly indeed . . . and from her regal bearing, she could be none other than the wasps' Queen.

There were several other wasps in the room tending her. Stripe buzzed something at them, and they slowly flew out.

Despite being so much larger than the insects, Twink suddenly felt very small. 'Oh, Stripe, why have you brought me here?' she whispered. 'If your

own doctors can't cure your Queen, why do you think *I* can?'

Stripe nudged her towards the bed. *Please, just try!* said his eyes. *I told her you would!*

Taking a deep breath, Twink moved to the bedside. The poor Queen looked even worse than she'd first thought. Her large, dark eyes were sunken, and her black and yellow stripes dull and faded.

'Hello, Your Majesty,' said Twink shyly. 'My name's Twink, and – and I'm here to try and help you.'

The Queen rolled her head towards Twink. Fairy and wasp regarded each other in silence. Twink bit her lip. The Queen looked so sad! Somehow she reminded Twink of someone – but who?

She pushed the thought aside. 'Um . . . can you tell me what's wrong?'

Chauncey-Oberon edged up beside her. 'She doesn't look very well, does she?'

Twink kicked him to be silent. 'Your Majesty, can you tell me what's wrong?' she repeated.

The wasp shook her head. To Twink's alarm, a

single tear rolled down her face.

'She doesn't seem very happy, either,' said Chauncey-Oberon. 'How are you going to help her? I mean – how are *we?*'

Twink resisted the urge to kick him again. The Queen did seem unhappy, but Twink was certain there was something else wrong. Yet she could see no injuries, and she hadn't a clue what sort of illnesses wasps might get.

Stripe was watching her imploringly. Twink fumbled with her box of fairy dust. 'Um . . . maybe a general perk-up spell,' she said.

Taking a pinch of the pink and gold dust, Twink clenched it in her fist and thought cheering, healing thoughts. When she could feel the magic tingling at her palm, she lightly tossed the glittering dust over the Queen.

'Does she look any better?' she whispered to Chauncey-Oberon.

'Not really,' he answered, making a face. 'Can't you do any better? This is hardly going to impress Queen Mab!'

Twink's wings went stiff with fury. Grabbing Chauncey-Oberon's arm, she yanked him away from the Queen's bed. 'You horrid, horrid boy!' she hissed. 'Don't you even *care* that she's so ill? No wonder your parents don't want to have anything to do with you!'

All the blood seemed to leave Chauncey-Oberon's face. Twink gasped. Oh, *how* could she have said such a thing? There was no excuse for it, no matter how angry she was.

'I'm – I'm sorry,' she said, her cheeks flaming. 'But we're not here to impress Queen Mab. We're here to *help*.'

Chauncey-Oberon's jaw was tight. Finally he gave a stiff nod. 'All right,' he muttered. 'Well – let's just get on with it, then.'

'But that's the problem, I don't know how!' burst out Twink. She glanced over her shoulder at Stripe, who was patting the Queen's arm soothingly.

'Chauncey-Oberon, what am I going to do?' she whispered. 'Stripe thinks I can help because I once healed a broken wing for him, but . . .' Twink trailed off helplessly. Whatever was wrong with the Queen, it was much worse than a broken wing.

Chauncey-Oberon gazed at the Queen and frowned. 'I wonder –' he started, and then broke off, his cheeks reddening. 'No, it's probably stupid.'

'What?' asked Twink.

He looked embarrassed. 'Well . . . when I was little, I had a pet ladybird. She was called, um . . . Dotty.'

His expression dared her to laugh, but Twink had never felt less like it in her life. 'Go on,' she urged.

Chauncey-Oberon hunched a purple wing. 'Well, Dotty got really ill once. My – my nurse said it was because she was worried about her children. She had heard that rhyme somewhere, about them all being in a fire.'

Twink nodded. They had learned all about that in Creature Kindness class, and how to cheer the poor ladybirds up if it happened. But when she said this to Chauncey-Oberon, he shook his head.

'No, you see Dotty *didn't* get cheered up, and so it got worse and worse. My nurse said she was heart-

sore – that her heart was actually making her ill from worry. And . . . it's probably stupid, but I think the wasp Queen looks sort of the same.'

Twink stared at him, her pulse pounding. Suddenly it came to her who the wasp Queen reminded her of: Queen Mab, when Twink had seen her from the courtyard. The same unhappy expression rested on both monarchs' faces – and suddenly Twink was certain she knew why.

She spun towards the bed. 'Stripe, when did your

Queen start to feel poorly? Was it after the meeting with Queen Mab?'

Flitting over to them, Stripe indicated that this was the case. At first their Queen had merely been unhappy that the meeting had gone badly, but a few days ago she had become seriously ill – and nothing their doctors could do had helped.

Twink knelt beside the wasp Queen's bed. 'Your Majesty, you feel just as awful as Queen Mab does, don't you?' she said. 'Because she *does* feel bad about what happened, I'm sure of it! She looked so sad the other day.'

The wasp Queen gazed up at her with disbelieving eyes. Heaving a sigh, she turned her head away. Twink swallowed. It was as if the Queen longed to believe her, but just couldn't bring herself to.

'Here, give me that fairy dust,' whispered Chauncey-Oberon. 'I'm going to try what my nurse did for Dotty.'

Taking a pinch of the pink and gold dust, Chauncey-Oberon held it in his hand. '*Sore heart*

mend, find a friend,' he murmured. Then, as Twink had done, he gently scattered the dust over the wasp Queen.

Twink leaned forward as the ill monarch stirred on her cushions. Was her colour slightly better? Twink thought it might be, but she couldn't tell.

'Here, let's both try it,' she said, reaching for more fairy dust.

Chauncey-Oberon blinked. '*Both* of us? But –'

'Of course!' cried Twink. 'Your nurse was an

adult; her magic was stronger than ours. But maybe together, we can do it.' She poured a bit of the fairy dust in his hand, and then held her own hand over it. Stripe watched them hopefully.

'All right,' said Chauncey-Oberon, looking doubtful. 'You have to think about her heart mending as you say the words.'

Twink nodded. Closing her eyes, she tried to imagine the wasp Queen's heart, picturing it whole and strong and healthy. '*Sore heart mend, find a friend,*' she murmured with Chauncey-Oberon. '*Sore heart mend, find a friend.*'

Together, they sprinkled the glittering fairy dust over the wasp Queen.

Chapter Eight

The magic dust swirled into a cloud and grew brighter, so that for several moments, they could hardly see the wasp Queen through the pink and gold sparkles. Twink held her breath.

Slowly, the dust faded . . . and Twink saw that the wasp Queen had drifted into a deep, healing sleep. A relaxed smile was on her face, and already her yellow and black colouring looked brighter.

Twink moved quietly away from the bedside, careful not to disturb her. Stripe followed with a soft, joyous buzz, flinging himself into her arms.

Twink hugged him tightly.

'Oh Stripe, I think she's going to be all right. I'm so glad!' She twirled them about in a circle. Suddenly she remembered Chauncey-Oberon. None of this would have been possible without him.

'*Thank you*,' she said, as Stripe nodded enthusiastic agreement. 'I would never have known what was wrong. You really *are* a hero – and I'll tell Queen Mab all about it. Your parents are going to be so proud of you!'

To her surprise, Chauncey-Oberon stiffened, and for a moment Twink thought he almost looked close to tears. Then he turned away with a scowl. 'Whatever. Come on, we've got to hurry.'

Twink's pink eyebrows drew together. What had she said to upset him? But there was no time to worry about it now. Chauncey-Oberon was right – they had to rush if they were going to make it back to the palace in time for their dance!

The journey back through the low-ceilinged corridors

seemed endless. Twink hurried along as fast as she could, but her legs and wings were soon aching worse than before.

'Are you all right?' she asked Chauncey-Oberon.

'Oh, leave me alone,' he said without looking at her.

Stung, Twink didn't reply. For a moment in the royal chamber, Chauncey-Oberon hadn't seemed bad at all – but now he was just as rude as ever. What was *wrong* with him, anyway?

Finally, they exited the palace and were flying up through the hollow tree again. Twink sighed with relief. How lovely it felt to stretch her muscles and feel the wind in her hair!

Chauncey-Oberon was flying behind her, clutching his left wing and grimacing.

'What's wrong?' asked Twink, swooping back to him.

'Nothing – I've got a wing cramp, that's all,' he retorted coldly. Cresting the rim of the hollow tree, they flew out into the wood. Stripe buzzed about them in concern.

'Is it a bad cramp?' pressed Twink. 'Because you really shouldn't fly with it if –'

'I said I'm fine!' shouted Chauncey-Oberon.

He put on a burst of speed, jetting away from her through the trees. As Twink watched in dismay, his left wing gave a shudder and stopped flapping. With an awful cry, Chauncey-Oberon fell towards the ground.

Twink darted after him. Hours of practice on the Glitterwings Fledge field had made her a strong flyer, and she managed to grab him as he hurtled to the ground.

'Get off!' yelled Chauncey-Oberon, struggling like the Fledge flea.

'Are you mad?' Twink fluttered wildly, straining to slow them both down.

Crash! They hit the ground in an explosion of autumn leaves and pine needles. Twink sat up with a groan. Ouch, her head! All at once she saw that Chauncey-Oberon had landed on his wing. 'Oh! Are you –'

The boy sat up. His bruised wing hung limply by

his side. 'Don't ask!' he snapped, his voice shaking. 'No, I'm *not* OK.'

Twink blew out a breath. Fine! She'd just keep quiet, since she couldn't say anything right.

Stripe buzzed up. Seeing Chauncey-Oberon's wing, he turned to Twink with a questioning expression. 'I suppose we're going to need some help getting back to the palace,' she admitted. 'Can you do anything, Stripe?'

He nodded, and flew quickly away.

Twink pulled her knees to her chest, wondering how much longer Stripe would be. He'd been gone ages already – they'd miss the dance at this rate!

Chauncey-Oberon's orchid and emerald suit was sadly battered from the fall, and looking down, Twink saw that her dress wasn't much better. She sighed. So much for looking like she belonged in the palace.

Suddenly she realised that Chauncey-Oberon was staring at her. 'What?' she said.

'What did you mean, *we* need some help?' he repeated slowly. 'Why don't you just fly back alone?'

'And leave you here?' said Twink in surprise. 'Of course not!'

'Why not?' demanded Chauncey-Oberon. 'You could be back in time for the dance. You could tell Queen Mab that *you* saved the wasp Queen, all on your own.'

'But I wouldn't do that,' said Twink in confusion.

Chauncey-Oberon glowered at the pine needle his feet were resting on. 'I would,' he said in a low voice.

'I don't believe you,' said Twink hotly. 'I don't think you're as awful as you make out – even if you *are* the rudest boy I've ever met! No one who helped the wasp Queen the way you just did could be *all* bad.'

Chauncey-Oberon fell silent, playing with a loose emerald on his suit. 'Nobody likes me, you know,' he said finally. 'Not even my parents. I hoped maybe they'd be proud of me if I did something amazing, but – but the truth is I was fooling myself. They'll never like me, no matter what I do.' He looked up, his eyes bright with tears. 'How did you find out?' he asked.

Twink's throat tightened. 'I – I'm sorry,' she faltered. 'I should never have mentioned it, not in a million years. But Chauncey-Oberon, I'm sure your parents like you! They're just really busy –'

He shrugged, wiping his eyes. 'How did you know, though?'

'Jay knows one of the boys at White Cloud,' confessed Twink. 'But no one was going to say anything to you! We all felt bad for you, even though –' She stopped.

'Even though I acted like a total moss brain,' finished Chauncey-Oberon. He leaned back against a stone and sighed. 'Nobody likes me, they never have,' he repeated. 'So I suppose I don't give them the chance any more. Why bother trying?'

'But of course you should bother!' exclaimed Twink. 'You need friends; everyone does.'

'Oh, it's easy for *you*,' said Chauncey-Oberon, throwing a pebble. 'Everybody likes you – I saw that right away, from the first moment we met! But what if you were me, and – and you never said anything right? And everyone teased you once they found out that your parents were never at home, and you lived with a *nurse*?'

'Do the other fairies tease you for that?' echoed Twink. 'But that's awful!'

Chauncey-Oberon made a face. 'They used to, at my old school. So now I just try to act more important than anyone else. My family *is* very important, you know, and – and sometimes it impresses the new boys, before they get to know me.' He looked down at the ground.

Twink's heart ached for him. But before she could say anything else, a buzzing noise reached their ears.

Stripe reappeared with a dozen other wasps, carrying a stretcher made of thick paper between them. Gently, the insects picked up Chauncey-Oberon and placed him on it.

The crimson-haired fairy went a bit pale. 'It looks like they're going to carry me back to the palace.'

The wasps lifted up the stretcher. 'I suppose it's the only way,' said Twink, fluttering beside him. 'Are you all right?'

Chauncey-Oberon nodded. 'But Twink — what will they *say*, when we arrive with a swarm of wasps?'

Twink swallowed. 'I suppose we'll find out,' she said weakly.

The wasps sped through the wood, carrying Chauncey-Oberon as lightly as if he were a leaf. Twink and Stripe flew just behind. Despite everything, Twink enjoyed spending time with her friend again. The two of them 'talked' the way they always had, swapping stories about what they'd been up to since they'd last seen each other.

All too soon, the royal clearing appeared through the trees. Twink's palms went damp as the wasps flew straight to the palace. As one, they dived through the leafy branches at the top of the bush.

The Queen's party was in full swing, with hundreds of grandly dressed fairies laughing and talking. Twink wasn't sure whether she and Chauncey-Oberon had been missed — but they certainly made their presence known now!

A shocked hush fell as the swarm of wasps carrying Chauncey-Oberon swooped over the fairies' heads, with Twink right behind them. One of the ladies screamed and ducked for cover.

'Sorry!' called Twink frantically over her shoulder.

'What's the meaning of this?' sputtered Maximus, bustling over as the insects set Chauncey-Oberon lightly on the ground. He scrambled to his feet, his hurt wing limp.

The wasps buzzed away through the branches with the empty stretcher – all except Stripe, who remained staunchly by Twink's side. Her heart

swelled. She knew how frightened her friend was of the fairies, but he wasn't going to leave her on her own.

'WHAT is the meaning of this?' repeated Maximus, red-faced. 'Miss Flutterby! Master Sparkworth! WHO is this wasp?'

Twink licked her dry lips. 'He – he's my friend,' she said. 'He needed help . . .'

Complete silence met her words as hundreds of adults stood gaping at them. Suddenly Twink was keenly aware of the sad state of her fine dress, and that one of her emerald combs was missing. Chauncey-Oberon lifted his chin, glaring haughtily.

'You'll have to explain more than that!' barked Maximus.

Twink's wings felt cold. 'Well . . . you see . . .'

Before she could say anything else, Queen Mab appeared, hovering over the crowd and touching down beside Twink and the others. The fairies all rose on to respectful tiptoe, inclining their heads.

Twink hastily did the same. She had thought the fairy monarch was beautiful before, but now she was

radiant – like sunshine! She wore a simple daffodil dress, and a crown with a single golden jewel in it.

'Please be at ease,' said the Queen. The crowd sank to its feet again. Twink gulped as the Queen regarded them closely.

'Would someone please tell me what has happened?' she asked.

In answer, Stripe buzzed forward. As the fairies watched in astonishment, the wasp began to act out the story – his friendship with Twink, his joy at seeing her again, his worry over the wasp Queen's illness – and his growing certainty that Twink might be able to help.

So beautifully did Stripe perform that everyone followed his story perfectly. The fairies watched, entranced.

All at once Twink spotted the other children, standing nearby. Though slack-jawed with amazement, none of them looked as if they thought any the worse of her for having a wasp as a friend. Tilli even caught Twink's eye, and smiled at her.

Relief rushed through Twink – but she was disappointed in herself, as well. She should have had the courage to tell them from the start. *I always will from now on*, she vowed. *Stripe's my friend, and I'm not ashamed to say so.*

The wasp was still telling his story. Chauncey-Oberon squirmed as Stripe mimed asking Twink and Chauncey-Oberon for help . . . and then described how the crimson-haired fairy was the only one who had known how to save the wasp Queen.

'But it wasn't like that at all!' Chauncey-Oberon blurted out. Stripe stopped, hovering in place.

'What do you mean?' asked Queen Mab. 'Is the wasp not correct?'

Chauncey-Oberon's face was poppy-red. 'No, he's just being nice. Your Majesty, I – I *made* Twink take me along, but only because I wanted to impress you. I didn't really care about helping the wasp Queen at all!'

'Perhaps not, but you are still the one who saved her,' pointed out Queen Mab gently. 'Is that not true?'

'I suppose, but –' Chauncey-Oberon scuffed at the ground. 'No, it was really Twink,' he admitted in a low voice. 'She had the idea of both of us trying the magic together. I would never have thought of that.'

'Ah!' said the Queen, smiling at Twink. 'Friends working together – great things can happen as a result. I am indebted to you both for saving my sister monarch. The two of us still have much to discuss . . . and much to learn from each other, if we can ever mend our bridges.'

There was a pause as the sadness returned to the Queen's face. She sighed. 'Our relations with the wasps are the reason why I requested the Friendship Dance today – and to be performed by school-children, for it was a child who first showed me that perhaps wasps and fairies *can* be friends.'

She nodded solemn thanks to Twink, who felt her cheeks catch fire.

With a graceful arm, the Queen motioned the other dancers forward. 'I don't know if the wasp Queen and I will ever see eye to eye, but I greatly wish for us to be able to. It is my dearest hope that magic might now succeed where diplomacy has failed.' She turned to Chauncey-Oberon. 'Are you well enough to dance?'

He nodded firmly, his injured wing still hanging by his side. 'Yes, Your Majesty.'

The Queen's gaze turned to the rest of the children. 'Then please . . . may we have the Friendship Dance?'

The dancers faced each other across the courtyard, just as Maximus had taught them. Twink saw the same worried look on every face. What if they made a mistake, and the magic didn't happen?

'And begin,' instructed Maximus. The cricket band struck up a graceful tune.

Twink started to dance. As one she and the others dipped and twirled . . . and as they performed the intricate steps, Twink could feel for the first time a slow, deep magic beginning to gather.

The dance brought them all together, girls and boys, with their various friendships criss-crossing like golden threads. The sparkle-seeker had done its job well, realised Twink. Each of them, through their friendships with each other, had brought something to the dance that was essential – even Chauncey-Oberon, by healing the wasp Queen!

As the eight of them danced and spun, Twink could feel the magic growing stronger. Suddenly bright, golden sparkles whirled around them, spreading out through the crowd like ripples in a pond. Faces relaxed as old friends clasped hands, and new ones smiled at each other.

Twink's heart skipped. The magic was working! But would it be enough to mend things between the two monarchs? *Oh, please, please let it help*, thought Twink fervently.

Finally the dance ended, and she dipped into a curtsy. Chauncey-Oberon bowed. An expectant silence fell over the courtyard as the last note from the cricket band faded away. Twink held her breath. She knew that everyone was waiting for the same thing: a sign that the wasps had felt the dance, too.

And then slowly, the magic began to fade – until it was as if the glow it had cast over the crowd had

never been there at all. The dancers exchanged an unhappy glance.

With a rustle of golden wings, Queen Mab flew forward. Though she tried to hide it, Twink could see the disappointment on her face.

'Thank you, you've all done very well,' she said softly. 'I – I suppose it was foolish of me to have such high hopes –'

She broke off at a sudden humming noise. The crowd gave a single loud gasp as the leaves above them parted and a small group of wasps appeared,

flying low over their heads.

'The wasp Queen!' someone cried.

It was really her! Twink caught her breath as the regal insect landed beside her, with several buzzing attendants in her wake. A small golden crown sat on her head, and there were tiny red jewels on her wings.

The wasp Queen nodded gravely to Twink and Chauncey-Oberon. *Thank you for healing me*, said her dark eyes. Then she looked at the other dancers. *And thank you, too.*

Suddenly Twink knew, beyond a doubt, that the magic had worked. She clasped hands tightly with Tilli. Stripe was hovering to one side, looking just as excited as she felt.

Queen Mab flew forward. 'Greetings, Your Majesty,' she said to the wasp Queen.

The insect monarch bowed her head. For a long moment, fairy Queen and wasp Queen regarded each other – two very different creatures who both longed for friendship.

'Thank you so much for coming,' said Queen

Mab, a smile beginning to spread across her face. 'We have a great deal to discuss – but for now, please join the party as an honoured guest.'

Hours later, Twink looked around the courtyard with a happy smile. The cricket band had started up again after the wasp Queen arrived, and hadn't let up since. The party had taken on a magic of its own as fairies and wasps danced together, cavorting long into the night.

And at the centre of it all, the two Queens sat side by side on a pair of richly carved chairs, deep in earnest conversation.

'You've done very well, my dear,' said Miss Shimmery warmly. As it turned out, Twink's HeadFairy had been at the party for hours, and had witnessed her arrival with the wasps – though she'd chosen not to interfere.

'Thank you,' said Twink, her cheeks turning pink. 'I – I know that Chauncey-Oberon and I shouldn't have gone off without telling anyone, but –'

'It can't have been an easy choice, but given the

circumstances I think it was probably the right one,' smiled Miss Shimmery. 'Now enjoy yourself, because tomorrow it's back to – *oh*!'

She broke off as Maximus, flushed from fizzy dew, spun her on to the dance floor. 'Come, Aurora, let's dance the night away!' he shouted.

Twink burst out laughing as she watched her HeadFairy and Maximus whirl away together under the shining crystals. What she wouldn't give for one of those human cameras, so that she could show all her friends back at school – they'd never believe her!

Tilli, Snow and Jena appeared through the crowd, with Stripe buzzing merrily above their heads. To Twink's delight, the other dancers had been glad to get to know her friend, with Snow in particular cooing over his soft, downy fluff.

'I can't believe it's almost over,' sighed Snow now.

Looking around, Twink remembered in amazement that she hadn't really wanted to come – and now she wouldn't have traded her time at the palace for anything.

'Oh, I'm going to miss you lot!' cried Jena, throwing her arms around them. 'I feel like you're my little sisters.'

'Yes, very little!' laughed Tilli, patting the diminutive Jena on the head.

'Show some respect for your elders,' said Jena, pretending to be offended. 'Isn't that right, Stripe?' The wasp buzzed loudly, bobbing in the air.

The boys came over then, and Twink saw that Chauncey-Oberon's wing had been bandaged by one of the Queen's doctors. 'Here,' he muttered, shoving a glass of sweet dew towards Twink. 'Um . . . can I talk to you?'

'All right,' said Twink in surprise, accepting the dew.

'I just wanted to say sorry,' blurted out Chauncey-Oberon when they were in a quiet corner of the courtyard together. 'I – I've been a real moss brain towards you, Twink. I've said some awful things over the last two weeks.'

'Well, what I said was pretty awful, too,' pointed

out Twink, remembering the terrible words she had flung at him in the wasp Queen's chamber.

'Yes, but at least *you* had a reason,' retorted Chauncey-Oberon. 'I didn't have one at all – I was just jealous. The Queen knew you instead of me, and – and you seem to make friends so easily, when I don't have any . . .' He trailed off, his pointed ears reddening. 'Anyway, I really am sorry,' he muttered.

'But you *do* have a friend,' burst out Twink. 'I

mean – I'll be your friend, Chauncey-Oberon, if you let me.'

His eyes widened, and then suddenly he smiled – a real smile, not a sarcastic one. It changed his whole face, and Twink found herself smiling back.

'Really?' he asked.

'Yes, of course!' said Twink. 'Besides,' she added, 'I don't see how we *couldn't* be friends, after all that's happened today.'

'No, I suppose not,' said Chauncey-Oberon. His smile grew even wider. 'You can't really go into a wasps' nest together and not become friends, can you?'

'Absolutely not!' laughed Twink.

'Will you write to me at White Cloud?' asked Chauncey-Oberon as they headed back to the party.

Twink nodded vehemently, her pink hair tumbling about her face. 'And you have to write to me at Glitterwings.'

'I will!' he grinned. 'I've never had anyone to write to before – it'll be glimmery.' Suddenly Chauncey-

Oberon ducked his crimson head. 'Um – can I just ask you one favour, though, Twink?'

'What is it?' she asked in surprise.

He smiled shyly as the party whirled around them. 'Would you call me Chaunce?'

To find out about other
glimmery Glitterwings
Academy stories, turn
over the page

Titania Woods

There are lots more stories about Glitterwings
Academy – make sure you haven't missed any of them!

If you have any difficulty in finding these in your local bookshop,
please visit www.bloomsbury.com or call 020 7440 2475
to order direct from Bloomsbury Publishing.

Visit www.glitterwingsacademy.co.uk for more fabulous fairy fun!